Mathilda
and the
Orange Balloon

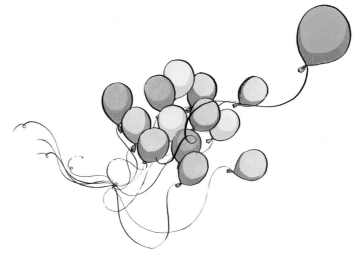

By Randall de Sève

Illustrated by Jen Corace

BALZER+BRAY
An Imprint of HarperCollinsPublishers

Balzer + Bray is an imprint of HarperCollins Publishers.

Mathilda and the Orange Balloon
Text copyright © 2010 by Randall de Sève
Illustrations copyright © 2010 by Jen Corace
Manufactured in China.

Library of Congress Cataloging-in-Publication Data
De Sève, Randall. Mathilda and the orange balloon / by Randall de Sève ; illustrated by Jen Corace. — 1st ed.   p.   cm.
Summary: When an orange balloon floats over her world of green and gray, Mathilda the sheep realizes that
she can be more than she is and sets out to convince the rest of the flock that anything is possible.
ISBN 978-0-06-172685-9 [1. Sheep—Fiction. 2. Balloons—Fiction. 3. Self-realization—Fiction.]
I. Corace, Jen, ill. II. Title.
PZ7.D4504Mat 2010   2008052108 [E]—dc22   CIP   AC

Typography by Carla Weise
10 11 12 13 14   LEO   10 9 8 7 6 5 4 3 2 1
❖
First Edition

For Peter, who lets me fly.
And in memory of Fred,
who insisted I could.
—R.D.S.

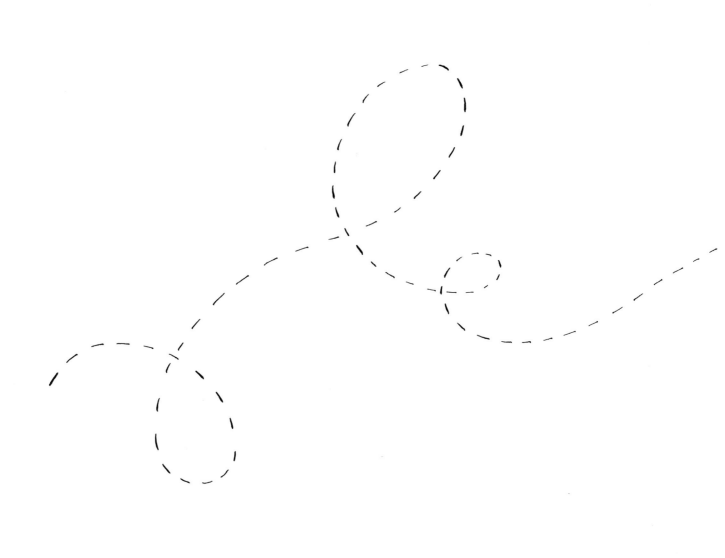

Mathilda's world was small.

Here's what was in it:

Green grass.

Green barn.

Gray skies.

Gray stones.

Gray sheep,

gray sheep,
gray sheep.

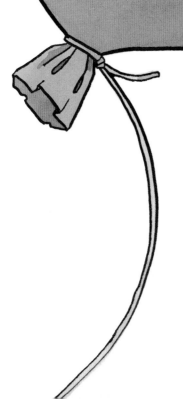

Which was all nice enough,
until the bright orange balloon floated by.

It caught Mathilda's eye while she was grazing.

Mathilda had never seen anything so magnificent.
At once, something inside her woke up.

"What was *that?*" she asked the others.
They were older and had seen such wonders before.
They barely looked up from the ground.

"Balloon," said a nearby ewe,
her mouth full of grass.

"Orange balloon," said another,
starting on a clump of clover.

"Orange balloon . . ." said Mathilda.
"That's me!"

"You?" The sheep laughed.
"You're not orange.
And you're not a balloon.
You're just a sheep.
And you'll always be a sheep."

Mathilda disagreed.

"Tell me," she said,
"what is an orange balloon?"

The sheep paused to think.
And to chew more grass.

"A balloon is round," one began.

"Go on," Mathilda said.

"And it flies," said another.

"Like this?" said Mathilda,
a little out of breath.

"Bah," the sheep replied.
"Anyhow, you're not orange."

"Really, what is orange?"

"Orange is tigers," said the sheep.
"Big and fierce."

"And?" Mathilda said.

"Orange is the sun," offered a lamb,
"warm as wool."

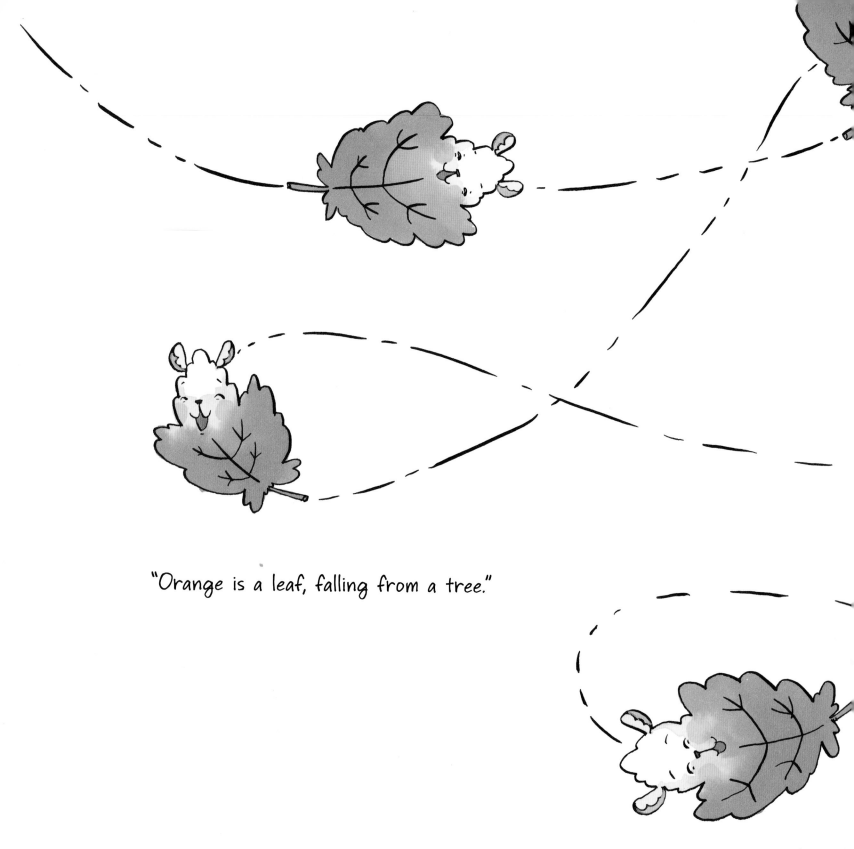

"Orange is a leaf, falling from a tree."

"And orange is happy," they all agreed.

Mathilda pictured herself
an orange balloon:
Round.
Flying.
Big and fierce.
Warm as wool. . . .

Happy.

Then the sheep realized—
anything was possible.

Especially with an orange balloon like Mathilda.